Daniel Says I'm Sorry

Adapted by Haley Hoffman
Based on the screenplay "Daniel Says I'm Sorry"
written by Jennifer Hamburg
Poses and layouts by Jason Fruchter

Simon Spotlight
New York London Toronto Sydney New Delhi

SIMON SPOTLIGHT
An imprint of Simon & Schuster Children's Publishing Division
1230 Avenue of the Americas, New York, New York 10020
This Simon Spotlight paperback edition December 2023
© 2023 The Fred Rogers Company
All rights reserved, including the right of reproduction in whole or in part in any form.
SIMON SPOTLIGHT and colophon are registered trademarks of Simon & Schuster, Inc.
For information about special discounts for bulk purchases, please contact Simon & Schuster
Special Sales at 1-866-506-1949 or business@simonandschuster.com.
Manufactured in the United States of America 1123 LAK
10 9 8 7 6 5 4 3 2 1
ISBN 978-1-6659-4764-0 (pbk)
ISBN 978-1-6659-4765-7 (ebook)

It was a beautiful day in the neighborhood, and Daniel Tiger was at school. "Vroom! Hi, neighbor! I'm playing with cars," said Daniel. But it wasn't a real car! It was a pretend car made out of cardboard.

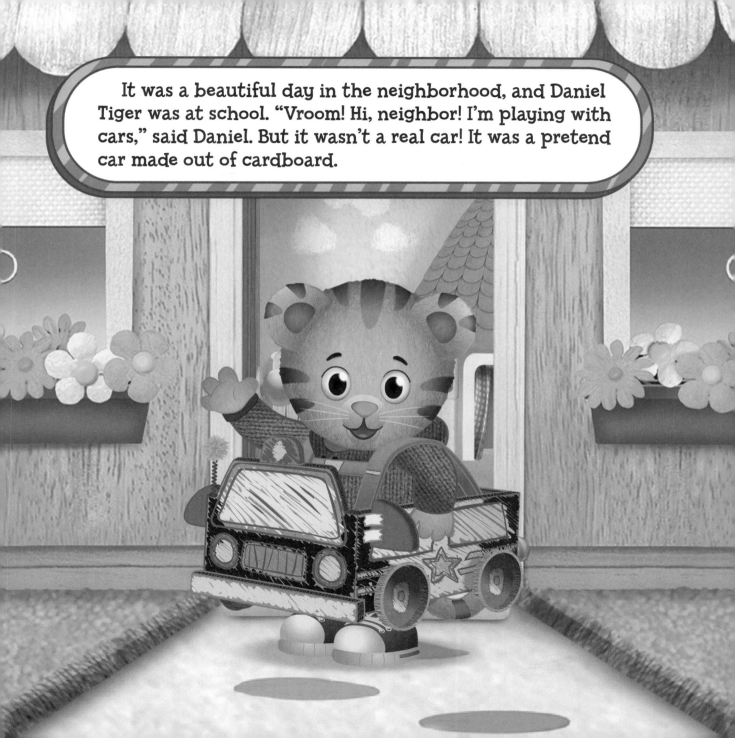

Daniel then played cars with Katerina Kittycat and Miss Elaina.
"Wee-oo, wee-oo. I'm a police car!" said Daniel Tiger.
"Ding, ding! I'm Trolley!" said Katerina.
"I'm a dump truck!" said Miss Elaina.

Miss Elaina tipped a container from her car and dumped out blocks. "Beep, beep, beep!" she said. "I'm dumping out toys . . . backward!"

Daniel imagined he was really a policeman helping animals cross the street.

"Go, policeman—driving up and down the street. Go, policeman! Go, go, policeman! A policeman helping animals cross the street. I'll get out of my car and hold my hand up in the street to help you. Go, policeman! Go, go, policeman!"

Daniel and his friends continued playing cars around the classroom. "Wee-oo!" said Daniel.

"Miss Elaina is too loud. And too close. And too . . . BEEPY!" said Daniel. He asked Miss Elaina to stop.

Miss Elaina saw that Daniel was upset. "What do I do?" she asked Katerina.

"Maybe you should say you're sorry," said Katerina.

Miss Elaina said she was sorry to Daniel, but he was still upset. Miss Elaina was confused. Why wasn't everything better after she said she was sorry?

Miss Elaina said she was sorry again. But this just made Daniel more upset. "Stop, Miss Elaina. Saying 'I'm sorry' isn't helping," Daniel said.

Teacher Harriet came over to help. "It's good that you said 'sorry,' Miss Elaina. But sometimes you need to do more than say 'I'm sorry.'" She sang,

"Saying I'm sorry is the first step.
Then, how can I help?"

Miss Elaina asked Daniel how she could help him feel better.
"Can you be quieter?" Daniel asked.
"Yes, I can be quiet! Like this . . . beep, beep, beep," said
Miss Elaina. Soon Daniel felt better and wanted to play again!

One of Katerina's wheels fell off. "You ripped my car costume, Daniel!" said Katerina.

Daniel looked at the broken costume. "Oh no, I didn't mean to do that. I'm sorry I ripped your car," he said.

"I am mad, meow meow!" said Katerina.
Teacher Harriet asked Daniel what he should do.
Daniel remembered,

♪ ♫ "Saying I'm sorry is the first step. ♪ ♪
Then, how can I help?"

Daniel asked Katerina how he could help her feel better.
"Can you help fix my car?" Katerina asked.
"Yes!" said Daniel. Daniel helped Katerina tape her car back together.

"You helped me fix my car! Thanks, Daniel!" Katerina said. She gave Daniel a big hug.